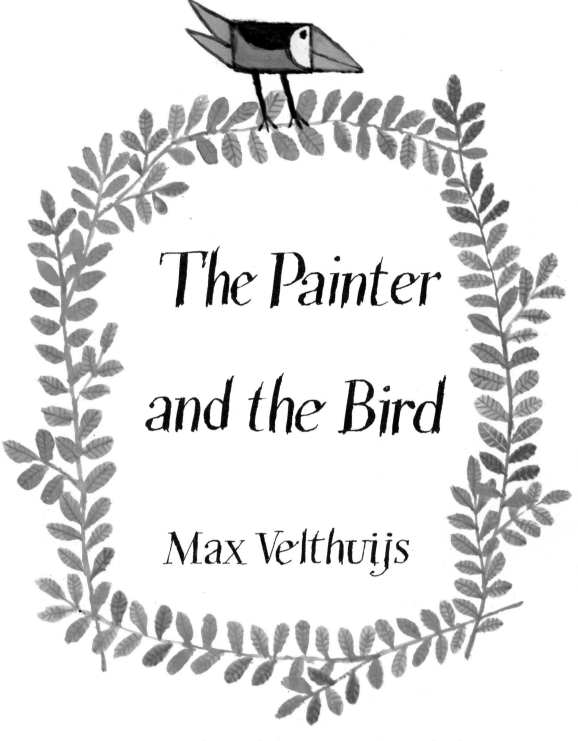

The Painter
and the Bird

Max Velthuijs

Translated by Ray Broekel

Addison-Wesley

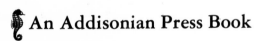 An Addisonian Press Book

First published in this edition 1975, by Addison-Wesley.
All rights reserved. No part of this book may
be reproduced in any form without the permission
of Addison-Wesley Publishing Company, Inc.,
Reading, Massachusetts 01867.
© 1971 Nord-Sud Verlag, Switzerland
Printed in Switzerland
First Printing

Library of Congress Cataloging in Publication Data:

Velthuijs, Max, 1923–
  The painter and the bird.

  SUMMARY: After an artist sells his favorite painting
of a bird, the bird becomes so homesick he flies out
of the picture and sets off to find his creator.
  "An Addisonian Press Book."
  Translation of Der Maler und der Vogel.
  [1. Fantasy] I. Title.
PZ7.V5Pai   [Fic]   74–8807
ISBN 0–201–08082–6

To those of us who have ever been lost or lonely

Once there was a painter. Like most painters, he was very poor. In his lifetime he had painted many beautiful pictures. He loved all his pictures. But he had one favorite. It was the picture of a strange and wonderful bird.

One day a rich man came to look at the painter's pictures.
He looked at all the pictures for a long time. And there
was one picture that he liked best of all. It was the painting
of the strange and wonderful bird. Of course, the poor painter
did not want to sell that painting. But the rich man offered
the painter more and more money. Finally the painter could
no longer refuse. The rich man paid for the painting
and took it away.

The rich man took the picture with him in his big red car. He took it to his beautiful house in the country. The picture was hung on the wall of the finest room, where the rich man could always enjoy looking at it.

But the strange and wonderful bird was not happy.
He missed the painter who had painted him.
And so, one day . . .
The picture bird flew away!

The picture bird flew out of the rich man's window and into
a field of flowers. In the field was a handsome rooster.
"Please," said the picture bird, "Can you tell me where
to find the painter who painted me? He is a kind man
and has a big beard." "Oh, I can't," said the rooster. "I don't know.
I never leave this field. Go and ask the birds in the forest.
They fly everywhere. Perhaps they can help you."

But the birds in the forest laughed at the picture bird.
"You really are a strange looking bird," they said.
"You belong in the zoo with all the other strange looking
animals. There is an animal in the zoo with a big beard.
Maybe he is the one you are looking for."

So the picture bird flew off to find the zoo. Soon the bird came to a large animal in a cage. The animal had a big beard. But it was a lion, not a painter.

"I am the king of the beasts," growled the lion. "When you sit on my head, you look like my crown. Why don't you stay for awhile? Perhaps your painter will come to paint my picture. Nothing would make a more beautiful picture than a lion with a crown on its head."

So the picture bird stayed in the zoo. And people came from everywhere to see the lion, king of the beasts, with the strange and wonderful bird sitting on its head.
But the painter did not come.

The director of the zoo looked out of his window. He saw the
lion with the strange and wonderful bird sitting on its head.
"Very interesting," said the director of the zoo. "I've never
seen a bird like that before. I will study it. This strange
bird will be named after me, and I shall become famous."
The director of the zoo took the picture bird to his office.
But he became so interested in reading his books about birds
that he forgot all about the picture bird.
So the poor picture bird flew away.

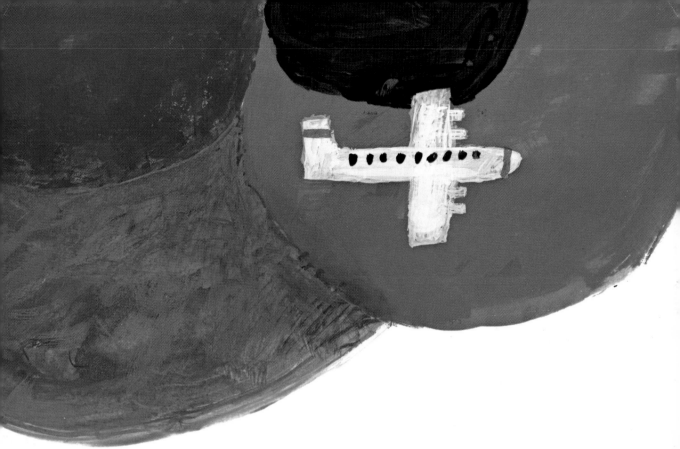

The sad picture bird flew and flew and flew. And it shed
a tear of unhappiness.
Then it saw something flying in the sky.
"Why that looks like a large white bird," thought the
picture bird. "Maybe it can help me!"
But the large white bird flew much too fast. It soon disappeared
into the clouds.

At last the picture bird could fly no more. It was tired.
It was lonely. It had no home. As it stood in the grass
with a big tear in its eye, along came a boy and a cat.
Fortunately for the bird, the boy arrived just before the cat!

The boy listened to the bird's story. And suddenly the boy remembered that he had seen the bird before.
"I know where you belong!" the boy cried. "I know where your friend the painter lives! Come along with me!"

At that very moment, who should appear at the painter's studio but the rich man. Under his arm was the painting he had bought. The rich man was very angry. He wanted his money back.

"You sold me a picture of a bird, but there is no bird in the picture!" shouted the rich man. So now the poor artist had no money, and no bird either!

Just as the rich man stormed out the front door,
the boy and the picture bird came in the back door.
The artist was overjoyed. He gave the boy a hug.
Smiling and laughing he said to the picture bird,
"WELCOME HOME!"
The picture bird, happy as could be, flew right back
to its place in the picture.

Then and there the painter promised never again to sell
the painting of the strange and wonderful picture bird.
The bird promised never again to fly away.
"I'll just pop out of my picture now and then, to stretch
my wings and to see how you are doing with your painting,"
said the bird.
And so the two friends lived together happily for the rest
of their lives.